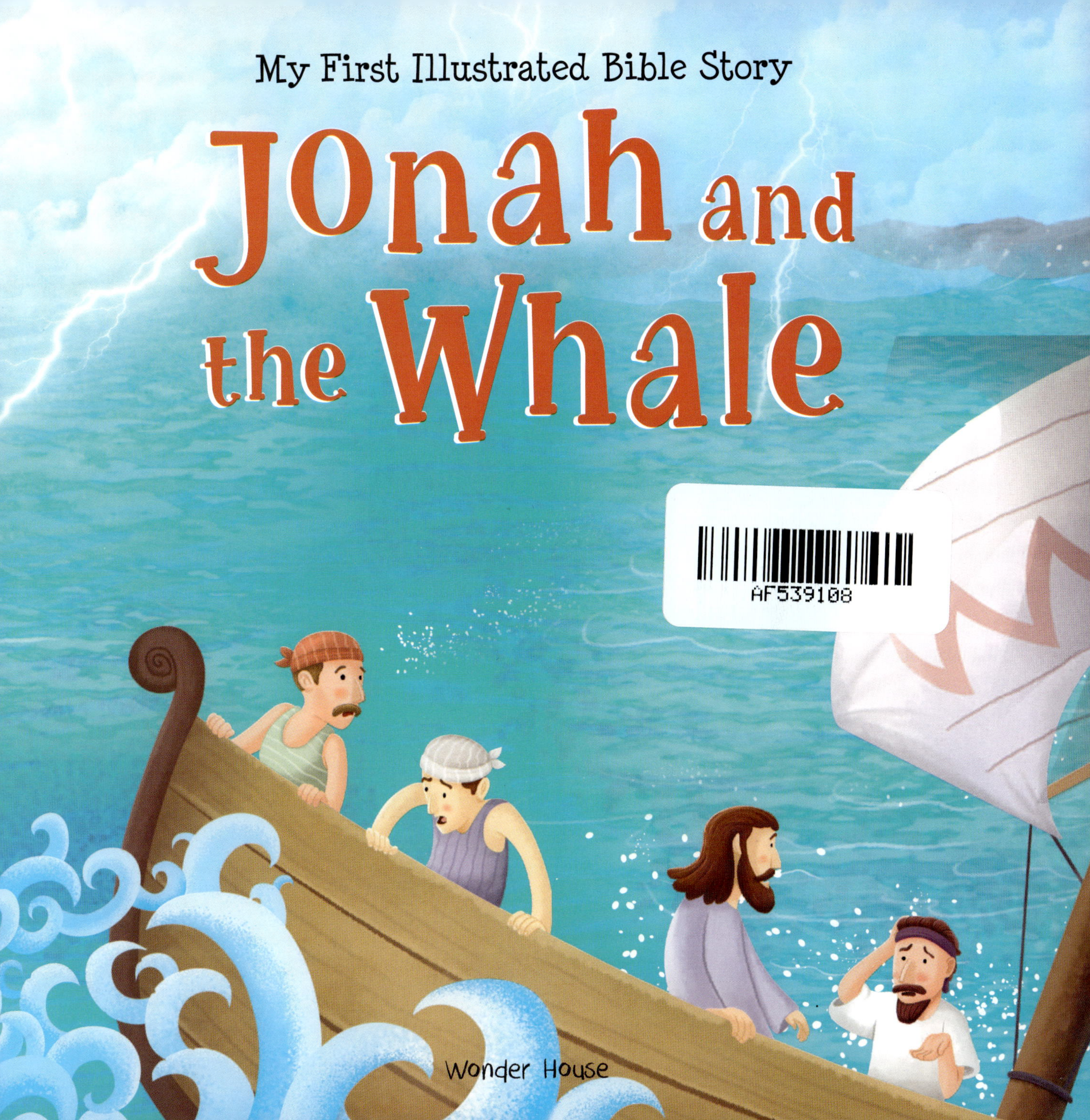
My First Illustrated Bible Story
Jonah and the Whale
AF539108
Wonder House

While the Syrian power was on the decline, a prophet, named Jonah, preached about God to the Israelites. One day God spoke to Jonah. He said, 'Go and preach in Nineveh.'

Jonah started the journey but when God saw him on the ship, he sent a great storm on the sea. The ship was tossed about on the waves. The sailors were terrified.

All this while, Jonah was fast asleep under the ship's deck. The ship's captain came to Jonah and said, 'Wake up! Pray to your God for safety.'

When the storm continued to rage, the sailors said, 'Someone on this ship has brought us ill-luck.' Jonah said that it was him. The next moment the sailors asked Jonah many questions—like who he was, where was he from, etc. Jonah quietly said, 'Throw me overboard. The storm will stop.'

But the sailor did not want to throw Jonah into the sea. But when the storm grew in intensity, they had no choice but to get rid of Jonah. Just then the storm ceased immediately.

As Jonah fell into the sea, a whale, sent by the God to rescue Jonah swallowed him. Jonah was alive inside the whale for three days and three nights. During this time, Jonah prayed to God and he made the whale throw up Jonah on land.

Once again, God asked Jonah to go to Nineveh. Jonah obeyed to the God's order. Once there, he cautioned people, 'Within forty days Nineveh shall be destroyed!'

The people of Nineveh believed this as the word of God. They turned away from their sins and started fasting.

The king of Nineveh kept aside his royal robes. He wore sackcloth, and sat amidst ashes. His people too turned away from sin. When God

saw that the people of Nineveh were repentant, he forgave them. This made Jonah very angry. He also feared that he might be called a false prophet as his prediction had not come true.

Jonah, then, built a small shelter outside the city and sat down to rest. Just then, God let a plant with thick leaves grow by the shelter to

shade Jonah from the sun. Jonah was grateful for the plant. A worm, however, destroyed the plant. Jonah was sorry that the plant had died.

It was then that the Lord said to Jonah, 'You are sorry to see the plant die, even though you had not planted or nourished it! Shouldn't I have pity on Nineveh, where so many people live?'

Jonah understood that all beings are precious to the God and should be saved.